AI, THE SILENT PARTNER OF OUR LIFE

AI AND US : RAISING THE FUTURE

RUPAL S. JAIN

This book is dedicated to every individual who is part of
this ever-evolving digital world. May this journey
empower us to raise the future with wisdom, compassion,
and purpose.

Contents

Preface

Artificial Intelligence has quietly become an integral part of our daily lives, enhancing and simplifying tasks behind the scene. As I navigated the challenges of parenting, managing my surroundings and connecting with people, I realized that many of us are unaware that we are already living in the age of AI. This realization inspired me to write this book. With my technical background, I felt I could help bridge the gap between technology and daily life in a practical, relatable way.

The book explores the role of artificial Intelligence in shaping the way we live, learn, work and connect.

This book serves as a valuable resource for modern parents, simplifying the complexities of raising children in today's world. The book also highlights on the challenges that we all may face in our daily life due to AI and proactive measures to safeguard themselves and their families from potential AI-related threats.

Hence, this book is meant to be an eye-opener for anyone who is, knowingly or unknowingly, influenced by AI. It explores how we can embrace the power of AI to improve our lives, while still holding on to the values that define us as humans.

Acknowledgements

Writing this book has been an enlightening journey of exploration and learning and I am deeply grateful to those who have supported me along the way.

First and foremost, I extend my heartfelt thanks to my respected parents and my elder sister who has given quality time to me and made me capable to put forth my thoughts into words which can really give insights to others. Next is my family including my husband and my kids for their unwavering encouragement and patience throughout this endeavour.

Special thanks to my family and friends to support and motivate me throughout the journey. Thanks to AI tools too in helping me coming out with presentable design. I am grateful to the publishing team for their professionalism and dedication in bringing this book to fruition.

Prologue

Today, in a quiet server room, machines process data at incredible speeds. They learn, adapt, and make decisions often without human help. This is not just science fiction. It's the reality of Artificial Intelligence (AI). From self-driving cars navigating city streets to algorithms predicting consumer behaviour, AI is seamlessly integrating into our daily lives.

As AI advances rapidly, a crucial question arises: What does it mean for humanity when machines can learn and evolve on their own?

This book highlights multifaceted world of AI, examining its influence on individual, its use in daily life, the benefits it presents and the challenges we face. We will also explore how AI is reshaping parenting, societies and our kid's intelligence growth.

As you turn these pages, consider this: AI is not just a tool we use; it impacts our values, our ambitions, and our fears. The journey ahead is not just about understanding AI applications but about understanding ourselves in an age where the line between human and AI is increasingly blurred.

CHAPTER ONE

JOURNEY FROM 'I' TO 'AI', ROLE OF 'I' IN THE WORLD OF 'AI'

'I' very important letter of our alphabet playing equally important role in our life. In early days, without involvement of 'I', no action or no task could complete. One had to physically present to do any task.

Now the world has changed. AI (Artificial intelligence) has come to our life. It has majorly replaced need of 'I' in performing any action. Hence power of 'I' is automated by AI. AI can do almost everything in our style, our way without our involvement.

AI: Reflecting you, replacing you.

Looks exciting, looks unbelievable but that's the AI all about.

Still the value that 'I' as an individual carry that 'AI' will not be able to deliver. Therefore, the future lies in a partnership between 'I' and 'AI'. By working together, we can combine human insight with technological expertise to achieve the best outcomes.

So now let's understand AI, the silent partner of our life.

AI, THE SILENT PARTNER OF OUR LIFE TODAY

Throughout history, we have seen that transformations are happening with time in the world around us. These changes happen gradually or suddenly, reshaping societies and cultures. This in turn influence our ways of living, our life style. Technology has been one of the most powerful forces shaping human history.

The invention of a computer and later the internet has transformed the way we live, communicate, and solve problems.

Technology is an invisible but invaluable silent partner for all of us.

In the digital age, technology has evolved at an unexceptional pace. Computers, smartphones, artificial intelligence, and automation have connected the world in just a click time. What once took centuries to change now happens in few seconds. Our ancestors struggled a lot in past for completing their tasks, for day-to-day routine, for talking to their near-ones at a distance. This generation who has not seen this struggle, efforts spent behind it seems unbelievable to them. As technology continues to evolve, it challenges us to adapt and ensure that progress benefits all of humanity.

Each transformation brings developments in all areas of life. Today, we are experiencing rapid technological transformations, especially with the rise of artificial intelligence and digital communication. These ongoing changes create new possibilities for all of us.

Transformation over time is not just about progress, it's about evolving to meet new challenges, learn from the past, and build a better future.

In this modern world we often juggle multiple roles. Every role that we perform requires varied skills and varied mindset. Many a times the environment too differ while being part of different roles. For example, a woman playing role of a mother in house and a role of a business woman in office.

In this balancing act, unknowingly technology has become a silent partner in our life and can help us streamline our tasks if used in a right way.

The technology has entered our world unnoticed. Still the influence of technology in our day-to-day task is major. Everything that we do from start of our day till we sleep, we knowingly or unknowingly use AI or technology somewhere. It has entered our life without making any noise. The outcome of being part of this technology world is amazing but challenges do exist. The way our homes and our offices operate has changed completely. Now a days due to remote working many offices infrastructure has vanished completely.

The silent partnership offers tremendous convince in terms of managing our schedules to enhancing our education.

Our perspective of looking AI as a partner rather than a tool helps us better integration of it in our daily life.

When we think of AI as a tool, we imagine a technology that we actively use to accomplish specific tasks, like a calculator for math or a hammer for building. In this role, AI performs functions on demand, under our direct control.

In contrast, viewing AI as a silent partner means recognizing it as an ongoing, behind-the-scenes collaborator in our daily lives. It operates quietly in the background: anticipating needs, adapting to our habits, and influencing decisions without us always being aware.

Use of technology in our day-to-day life helps us balance our home and career responsibilities. The shift towards digital world accelerated by the pandemic has opened many doors for all of us. Let's explore more and know how this technology, a silent partner can be used wisely to enhance our daily routine.

AI has woven itself into the fabric of daily existence.

AI has influenced all age groups starting from children, youngsters to senior citizens. AI has entered in the world of education, work, relationships, and even parenting.

Hence now we will see how AI has unknowingly changed life style especially childhood life and how do we work with it as a successful partner to maintain our identity, values, and the future we are shaping—not only for ourselves but for the next generation.

CHAPTER THREE

11

AI - ENHANCED CHILDHOOD

Yes. AI has impacted every individual's life style but major impact is on growing child.

Childhood is a very important stage of life. It builds the base for how we grow, learn, stay healthy, and interact with others. Today's children are tomorrow's leaders. That's why it's important to give them good values and a supportive environment while they're still young.

In the past, children learned mainly through real-life interactions with parents, teachers, and friends. They used books, blackboards, and hands-on activities. Information was found in libraries or taught in classrooms. Kids played outside, used their imagination, and did arts and crafts.

Today, things are changing with the arrival of AI (Artificial Intelligence). AI Tools help children learn quickly and in a way that fits their needs. There are many educational apps, games, and AI tutors. Kids now have access to tons of information online. They also connect with others through social media and digital platforms. Playtime now includes video games, virtual reality, and AI-powered games.

AI is beneficial to children in a way that it can make learning more personal, help them improve communication skills and built many more skills with online channels. It can even help children in remote areas by giving them better learning tools. However, there is lot of risk involved. AI collects personal data and if not handled carefully, that data could be misused. Also, if kids depend too much on technology, they might miss out on real-world experiences, which can affect their social and emotional development.

That's why,

It's important to find the right balance. Parents and teachers need to guide children on continuous basis. AI can support learning and growth, but it must be used wisely and ethically, with attention to children's overall well-being.

KIDS: OUR REFLECTION, OUR VALUES

In AI world, role of parents is very vital.

To understand how to induce values in our kids, let us first understand our kids in today's world.

<u>*Kids Our reflection, Our responsibility*</u>

Can we spare sometime and go back to our childhood....

*The **fun days** we had, **stress-free environment** we lived, **friend circle** we had, level of **communication** we had with our family, **games** we used to play with our parents and lot many things.....*

We did not have so many exposures but, the freedom (stress-free) to play and study.

We did not have many activities around but, exposure with no competition around.

We did not have too many tuitions but, still have professionals and skilled people around.

Feel so nice to think of all this.

BUT Are we as parents really providing the same environment to our kids?

They are always loaded with too much of competition, too many challenges, too many exams and evaluations, too many tuitions. It's an environment full of stress. It is good sometimes to have competition but everything in excess is harmful. Parents, it's taking away their childhood.

CHILDHOOD COMES ONLY ONCE

LET's NOT SPOIL IT...

LET THEM ENJOY AND EXPLOTE

AT THEIR OWN PACE.

Today's child can very well handle competition and challenges so do not worry much about it. They are firm, they are brilliant. They learn and implement things faster than us.

Education is important but it should not come at the cost of happiness and mental well-being.

The formula is very simple. What we have is what we give to the world. Today's generation has stress, competition, challenges so what we will get in reverse would be the same. And that situation would be difficult to handle in future. To ensure that we do not spoil our kid's childhood, give them stress-free environment to live and make our future a better time to live with them, let this be an eye-opener.

SO,

Let's work towards nurturing and teaching our child values of life, kindness, honesty, love, communicate with them, spend quality time with them, keep them engaged in good networks and help them be a good human being. Rather than focusing too much on all kinds of extra-curriculum activities which may not be of any interest to them. Let's respect their view, their interest, give a pause and understand them.

We are blessed with technology, let's use it to its fullest and induce good values in our child in the way they love to learn. Let's praise them for what they are and teach them to praise others too.

Kids are reflection of our values,

they are reflection of God's pure love and beauty of life.

By loving and guiding them

we honour God's most beautiful creation.

Give a pause and think over it..

CHAPTER FIVE

AI – PARENTING THE CHAPTER REVISITED

As mentioned before, we have seen that transformations are happening with time. Due to transformations, Infrastructure is getting reshaped, Fashion gets revised with time, even our academic syllabus, our text books get revised with time.

These revised chapters of life we accept as it comes, then,

why don't we think that few chapters of Parenting need to be revised too with time.

Gentle Parenting:

Approach: Gentle Parenting

In today's fast-paced and technology-driven world, the traditional method of raising children which emphasized more on discipline and strict attitude need to get evolved into more understanding and flexible approach. The shift from rule-based to gentle parenting has to happen.

Instead of complaining, try to understand our child. During any conversation with teacher or friends or our child, all negative comments should be listened carefully and worked towards improving it. Let it not go into angry or arguing mood, they are our well- wishers.

Parenting : Use of Technology

<u>*Parenting Approach - Use of Technology*</u>

Earlier kids were not much aware of external world, opportunities and resources were limited. Now the world is getting smaller day by day. Opportunities are many, it is a matter of catching it at the right time, resources are huge due to internet coming in life.

Internet can play a major role in parenting now a days. Parents have plenty of data of their child's education, academic performance, school and behavioural records. Analysis of these data should be done to identify their Strengths and Weakness instead of pushing them into competitive world.

Lot of information is available with parents to educate their children that too at their comfortable time and at home too.

Challenges like screen-addiction, social media access, digital influence needs to be controlled by parents. This is a big challenge now a days for parents. But can be managed by spending more quality time and increasing level of communication with them since beginning.

Parenting : balancing work and home life

<u>Parenting - Balancing work and home life</u>

Now a days life style is costly, level of competition is more so both parents are sometimes working. This needs balance in work-home life. Raising children in this life style with good values is again a challenge for parents.

Spending quality time, engaging kids in religious or good networks or social events will surely help overcome this situation also. Story telling at night time etc can also help to prepare for enrolling them into this kind of activity.

Parenting : In nuclear family

Parenting - Nuclear Family

Now a days shift from joint to nuclear families lead to change in raising pattern of children. For teaching the holistic values parents rely more on schools and extra activities. Parents are more concerned about children's mental well-being too.

Actions speak more than words,

so, our life style, our behaviour with family-friends will teach big lessons to the child. Respect grandparents and having them with us will add much more values to children's upbringing. Their experience, their love will re-shape childhood of our child. Keep family-reading time, family-playing time more. When kids are small focus more on making him a good person instead of great person.

Good person with great values will surely be a great personality of future one day.

Parenting : In competitive world

<u>Parenting Approach: In competitive world</u>

Do not load him/her with too many activities, give them time to play with friends and family. Teach your child to even lose at times.

Now with so many challenges for parents, in brief the simple approach as per my view is,

- *Our life style needs to be revisited*

- *Raising level and quality of communication with kids*

- *Focus more on value-building (Outcome would automatically been seen in long run)*

- *Engage in religious activities*

We need to come out of complaining phase and start improving the situation making best use of technology in an alert way.

AI : Friend or Foe In Youth Life

AI has majorly influenced youngsters. Their life style is totally going digital. They are the people who cannot imagine the world without technology, without AI. AI is woven in their life completely.

AI has both positive and negative impact on their life. Education, health care, social interactions, bonding with family and friends, corporate-world, life-style and many more major areas are impacted by AI. This teenagers are those who are totally aware of AI world technically too. But as AI is making their activities easy-going, they make a choice to use it completely everywhere.

It is good for this generation to use it to grow. This generation can benefit from using technology to flourish but at the same time they are the people who need to be extremely conscious about it's after effect and risk.

Mis-understanding and over-understanding are the two areas of concern in the world of AI communication.

With time they are losing bonding with family and friends too as the level of communication is reducing amongst all day-by-day.

This generation need to understand and use technology as a partner to make bright and successful future.

CHAPTER SEVEN

AI – Friend or Frustration for Our Elders

AI has impacted a lot in the life of our senior citizens, our elders. It provides immense promise for improving their lives by offering benefits to enhance their health and safety.

At the same time, excessive use of technology in the house which has completely replaced old traditional model of life style brings uncomfort to them. Today we see that they are also trying to learn and use technology to the extent possible.

This technology can be used to empower seniors and help them live longer, healthier, and more fulfilling lives.

Help our elders feel comfortable in today's world and try to be in their world too sometime to bring a SMILE on their face.

CHAPTER EIGHT

AI - Know your Challenges in AI world

Challenges lie in maintaining our valuable skills, shaping our kid's future in AI world, misuse of AI by experts and hackers and lot more.

The first challenge is maintaining our **Reading, Writing** *and* **Memory skills.**

Reading: Shift from BOOKS to SCREENS

AI - Shift from BOOK to SCREEN

Reading is considered as Fuel for brain and Food for the soul.

But now a days habit of reading a book in-fact habit of reading itself is reducing. The technology transformation has changed the way people consume knowledge. Now a days people scan internet, watch videos and ask for information on instant messaging. This kind of reading has reduced patience and focus. It makes deep reading less common.

Reading is an art. Don't let it vanish.

Benefits of reading are many, as we all know-

<u>**Benefits of Reading a physical book**</u>

- It **<u>enhances</u>**knowledge, sharpens the mind, and fuels creativity.

- Reading a story book and watching story on internet has a big difference in terms of **<u>imagination and creativity</u>** that our mind develops.

- Studies suggest that reading regularly can **<u>reduce stress</u>**, **<u>improve cognitive function, and even prevent mental decline in old age</u>**.

- Reading is a **<u>Lifelong Companion</u>**. Book is said to be one of **<u>our best friends</u>**. Reading is not just a habit or an exercise—it is an essential part of life.

The decline in reading habit, be it a physical book or online reading itis a real concern in *today's world. This will make coming generation lose ability to think critically, think deeply and lose to develop patience.*

So here are few points that we can do now.

<u>Start Early with Storytelling.</u> Even before a child learns to read, parents can introduce them to books through storytelling. <u>Create a Reading-Friendly Environment.</u> Keep books accessible by having a small bookshelf at the child's eye level. Encourage children to pick books they find interesting. <u>Be a Role Model:</u> Parents are role model for children. They imitate parent's habits. If they see adults reading regularly, they are more likely to develop an interest in books. <u>Set a Reading Routine.</u> Establish a daily reading time.

Book, A friend forever

In a digital world filled with distractions, making time for reading can be one of the most rewarding investments in one self.

Writing : AI a game changer, BUT...

AI : A Game changer for writing Skills

As far as writing skills are considered, AI (Artificial Intelligence) has almost replaced human involvement.

*It too has many areas of concern. Writing skills require combination of **cognitive, linguistic** and **creative skills.** It requires **coordination of brain, eye and hands.** Brain which generates and organizes ideas, eyes that guides hand movements and helps in maintaining proper formatting and hands which controls pen for handwriting.*

Writing is a complicate process which requires multiple skills to get the effective outcome.

AI, a Writer

AI has made our work faster, very less efforts required in coming up with right contents for right audience with right style of presenting (including visual presentation) in a fraction of seconds. Yes, this is a breakthrough. Strengths of AI is its speed, precision and scalability.

The tools generated by human beings are acting smarter than humans.

But as per my view, human is God's creation and no-one can replace god's beautiful creation. I think robots will never replace humans but will surely replace efforts made by humans. God has given human a gift of emotions, feelings, unlimited brain power, creativity, imagination and many more. These things in true sense might not be possible to achieve by AI.

It's good that our education system has so far not allowed children to use AI as part of academic exams and evaluation. Believe me friends, anyways we are not using more than 2% of our brain and if we start using AI completely, we will stop using even that too. If we do not use AI just as a tool, in near future

Humans will than act like robots and Robots will act like humans...

So, use AI but keep writing and let kids also learn to write. Here are some ways in which we can still keep ourselves engaged in writing.

Prepare To-do list everyday this will help plan your routine and keep your writing habit part of a daily routine. Let kids make hand-made greetings cards in family occasions. Involve kids in hand-writing competitions. Explore Calligraphy to kids. Writing once is as good as reading the same content almost ten times in terms of memorizing it.

Hand writing can describe personality so explain them importance of hand written skills. Keep checking notebooks of your child and help them work towards improving them. Teach them multiple languages at least mother tongue, research says that brain has significant capacity in learning languages and learning multiple languages can restructure the brain to enhance its abilities.

It's a balance that we need to make, use technology as a tool in writing while maintaining criticality and originality in writing to oneself.

*Keep our brain engaged and let's move in
hand-in-hand with AI world.*

Maintaining OUR Memory in the Technology World

AI World : Maintain Our Memory Skills

*Scientists have discovered that our memory capacity isn't fixed but rather malleable like plastic (**Neuroplasticity**). In today's digital era technology has transformed the way we store, access and calculate our information. The traditional methods of maintaining and memorizing data has almost vanished.*

*The way we used to maintain **phone diary**, **write notes**, **maintain folders** of important documents, store **educational records in a file** was completely a difference experience. Now we have lots of data available easily in almost no time. However, while technology offers convenience, it also raises concerns about <u>memory retention and cognitive abilities</u>.*

*Today smart devices have led to a phenomenon known as **<u>digital amnesia</u>** (a dependency on technology for remembering information instead of using our own cognitive skills).*

As we increasingly rely on digital tools, it is essential to keep our memory intact so that we do not lose to retain and recall information effectively, at least information we need in emergency (few phone numbers or addresses etc).

Strategies to Maintain Memory in a Digital Age:

AI - Memory management

1. Consciously limiting dependency on Digital Devices

•

Reducing over-dependency on technology.

•

Don't turn to google immediately, make a solid attempt with your mind to retrieve information yourself.

•

Encouraging mental exercises like solving puzzles and playing memory-enhancing games can also be beneficial.

•

Learn and teach kids speedy Indian calculation technologies like Vedic Maths, ABACUS etc instead of using computer.

~

2. Maintaining a Healthy Lifestyle

•

Memory function is closely linked to <u>overall health</u>.

•

Regular physical <u>exercise</u>, a balanced <u>diet</u> rich in brain-boosting nutrients, adequate <u>sleep</u>, and <u>stress management</u> contribute significantly to memory retention

3. Learning new skills everyday

•

Memory strength is just like muscular strength. Learning a new skill is an excellent way to strengthen our brain's memory capacity.

•

Engage yourself in reading books or writing journals.

•

Once learnt, repeat and recall aloud or write it down. Repetition reinforces the connections we create between neurons.

This will help you remember learnt concepts for long term.

Do not allow technology to weaken our memory. Technology enhances the efficiency but use it to enhance our memory skills too.

AI - The Silent Threat:

Every coin has two sides. Similarly, if AI is Misused, it can disrupt our daily lives. The rapid advancement of AI brings numerous benefits but also significant risks when misused.

AI can be exploited to bypass security systems and can lead to important secured data hacking. AI-generated deepfakes can produce realistic but fake audio and video content, leading to misinformation, financial fraud, and damage to reputations. AI-powered autonomous weapons can do potential damage. The automation of jobs through AI leads to unemployment and particularly affecting low-skilled or old traditional process skilled people. There are many more such threats which will rise with time as AI advances.

The only way out of being proactive is, understand before you respond.

Do not use AI blindly, educate yourself enough to live in AI world, be it any age group.

Teach and explain your kids about AI threats too. Once you land up in any such troubles, know steps to take further to start taking actions on it.

so, see to it that,

YOU ARE NOT DRIVEN BY AI

BUT,

YOU ARE THE ONE DRIVING IT.

Let control still be with you. This is the only way to reduce risk of AI threats.

CHAPTER NINE

THE HUMAN ELEMENT: MAINTAIN IN AI WORLD

The Human Element, the must element in one's life, is very essential. Let us see to it that in near future AI does not take away this element from us. Even though we have social media platforms, online applications, do meet your friends and family occasionally.

Human element is required for us as it provides emotional support and qualities which AI can never think of.

Empower 'i' In The Age Of 'ai'

As AI continues to evolve, its influence impacts all age groups and various sectors, from healthcare and education to finance and transportation. While AI offers unprecedented opportunities for innovation and efficiency, it also presents challenges, particularly concerning kid's growth, parenting, employment and maintaining our valuable skills.

Use AI as a partner with a mindset that future AI should not completely rule human but help to reach our goal in easy and effective way.

Our senior citizens should not feel helpless in the world of AI today so do keep using our traditional life style in our routine and make them comfortable in current life style.

SO, to empower 'I' in the age of 'AI' ensure that:

AI DOES NOT CONTROL YOU COMPLETELY.

BUT,

YOU DRIVE THE AI IN THE WAY YOU WANT.

AI IS EVOLVING EVERY MOMENT

and SO MUST WE.

TO GROW and STAY CONNECTED,

WE NEED TO CONTINUOUSLY

LEARN and ADAPT WITH TIME.

65

THANK YOU